USHA WAS THE DAUGHTER OF THE NOBLE ASURA KING, BANA OF THE THOUSAND ARMS.

BANA WAS A DEVOTEE OF LORD SHIVA. ONE DAY WITH HIS THOUSAND ARMS, HE PLAYED VARIOUS MUSICAL INSTRUMENTS AS SHIVA DANCED THE TANDAVA.

SHIVA, IMMENSELY PLEASED, GRANTED HIM A BOON.
FOR THE PLEASURE YOU HAVE GIVEN ME, I ASSURE YOU OF MY PROTECTION.

BUT AFTER SOME TIME BANA BECAME VAIN AND COMPLAINED TO SHIVA.
MY THOUSAND ARMS ARE BECOMING A USELESS BURDEN TO ME.
EVEN WITHOUT THEM THERE IS NONE EQUAL TO ME, SAVE YOU.
SHIVA, TO PUT AN END TO THIS, CURSED HIM.
O VAIN AND FOOLISH ONE, IN A FUTURE ENCOUNTER, ONE EQUAL TO ME, WILL HUMILIATE YOU.
BUT BANA WELCOMED THE CURSE AND LOOKED FORWARD TO MEETING A PEER IN FIGHT.

A FEW DAYS LATER, USHA AND HER FRIENDS WERE PICKING FLOWERS IN THEIR FAVOURITE GROVE.
IT'S GETTING WARMER AND OUR BASKETS ARE NEARLY FULL.
YES. I'M TIRED. LET'S REST.
THEY SET THEIR BASKETS DOWN AND LAY DOWN UNDER THE TREES.
AS USHA DROWSED, SHE HAD A DREAM.

USHA WOKE UP WITH A START.
LORD! WHERE ARE YOU ?
HER FRIENDS WERE AT FIRST STARTLED...
... AND THEN AMUSED. THEY BEGAN TEASING HER.
WHERE IS WHO ? TELL US, USHA. DON'T BE SHY.
WHO IS THIS LUCKY LORD, WHO HAS WON YOUR HEART ?
BUT CHITRALEKHA, THE DAUGHTER OF ONE OF BANA'S MINISTERS AND USHA'S CLOSE COMPANION, CAME TO HER RESCUE.
HUSH! LEAVE HER ALONE. BE OFF WITH YOU.

WHEN THE OTHERS HAD GONE, SHE TURNED TO USHA.
WHOM ARE YOU LOOKING FOR, O PRINCESS?
USHA DECIDED TO CONFIDE IN HER.
A CERTAIN PRINCE CAME TO ME IN MY DREAM.
I WANTED TO KEEP HIM WITH ME. BUT HE DISAPPEARED LEAVING ME IN GRIEF.
WHO WAS HE?
I DON'T KNOW. HIS SKIN WAS DARK BLUE AND HE WORE YELLOW GARMENTS.

CHITRALEKHA CONSOLED HER.
DO NOT GRIEVE, MY PRINCESS. IF THIS PRINCE EXISTS, I CAN AND SHALL BRING HIM TO YOU.
BUT FIRST YOU WILL HAVE TO IDENTIFY HIM FOR ME FROM AMONG THE MANY PORTRAITS I SHALL PAINT FOR YOU.
CHITRALEKHA FIRST PAINTED A NUMBER OF GODS ...
IS HE ONE OF THESE?
NO!

... GANDHARVAS ...
OR THESE?
NO!
... AND YAKSHAS.
PERHAPS THESE?
NO!
THEN WHEN AMONG THE VARIOUS PORTRAITS SHE PAINTED KRISHNA AND HIS SON PRADYUMNA —
IS HE EITHER OF THESE?
NO! BUT ...
USHA WAS ABASHED, BECAUSE THEY RESEMBLED CLOSELY THE PRINCE OF HER DREAM.

AT LAST CHITRALEKHA DREW THE PORTRAIT OF ANIRUDDHA, SON OF PRADYUMNA. USHA, SUDDENLY SHY, CAST HER EYES DOWN.
THIS IS HE !
HE SHALL SOON BE HERE WITH YOU.
I SHOULD HAVE KNOWN ! SURELY, AMONG MEN, IT COULD ONLY HAVE BEEN ONE OF THE VALIANT YADAVA RACE WHO COULD HAVE DISTURBED MY PRINCESS.
THEN CHITRALEKHA WITH THE HELP OF HER YOGIC POWERS CONVEYED HERSELF...

... TO DWÀRAKA ...
... AND INTO THE PALACE OF ANIRUDDHA.
SHE FOUND HIM FAST ASLEEP ON HIS BED.
I AM FORTUNATE. I SHALL DO WHAT I HAVE COME TO DO BEFORE HE WAKES UP AND RESISTS.

THUS, WHILE ANIRUDDHA SLEPT, CHITRALEKHA, USING HER YOGIC POWERS, TRANSPORTED HIM TO THE KINGDOM OF BANA...

...AND INTO THE PRESENCE OF HER DEAR PRINCESS, USHA.
HERE HE IS, MY PRINCESS. HE IS YOURS.

USHA WAS DELIGHTED.
DEAR CHITRALEKHA, YOU HAVE BROUGHT ME GREAT HAPPINESS. I SHALL EVER BE GRATEFUL TO YOU.

CHITRALEKHA WENT AWAY, LEAVING USHA WITH ANIRUDDHA.
WHERE AM I ? WHO ARE YOU ?
I AM USHA, THE DAUGHTER OF BANA. MY LOVE FOR YOU HAS BROUGHT YOU HERE TO THIS PALACE AS MY HONOURED GUEST.
YOU HAVE BEEN BROUGHT HERE IN SECRECY AND...
...YOU ARE FREE TO LEAVE IF YOU SO DESIRE.

BUT ANIRUDDHA WAS NOT ABLE TO TAKE HIS EYES OFF THE LOVELY USHA.
I CANNOT DREAM OF LEAVING YOU. I WOULD RATHER STAY HERE AND DELIGHT IN YOUR COMPANY.
THUS IMPRISONED BY THE TENDER ATTENTIONS OF USHA, ANIRUDDHA MARRIED HER.
SHE ENTERTAINED HIM WITH SONG AND DANCE ...

... AND FED HIM WITH THE CHOICEST OF FOODS AND THE SWEETEST OF WORDS.
IN MY DREAMS YOU HAUNTED ME. IN FLESH AND BLOOD YOU SPIRIT ME AWAY.

ANIRUDDHA LOST COUNT OF THE DAYS.
I'VE WON AGAIN!
YOU ARE AS CLEVER AS YOU ARE BEAUTIFUL.

BUT SUCH STOLEN HAPPINESS COULD NOT LAST FOR EVER ONE DAY—
IT IS STRANGE ! THE PRINCESS HARDLY STEPS OUT OF HER ROOMS.

PERHAPS SHE IS ILL !

NO ! I SUSPECT...
HUSH! LET US SEE FOR OURSELVES BEFORE WE SUSPECT ANYONE OF ANY-THING.

THE ATTENDANTS THEN SPIED ON THE PRINCESS.

THEY WENT STRAIGHT TO BANA.
O KING, FORGIVE US. WE ARE AFRAID THAT YOUR DAUGHTER'S CONDUCT...
WHAT DO YOU MEAN? SPEAK OUT.
SHE HAS SECRETLY MARRIED THE YADAVA PRINCE, ANIRUDDHA.
WHAT!
OH LORD, WE ARE AT A LOSS TO UNDERSTAND HOW YOUR DAUGHTER WHO IS NOT ALLOWED TO MOVE ABOUT...

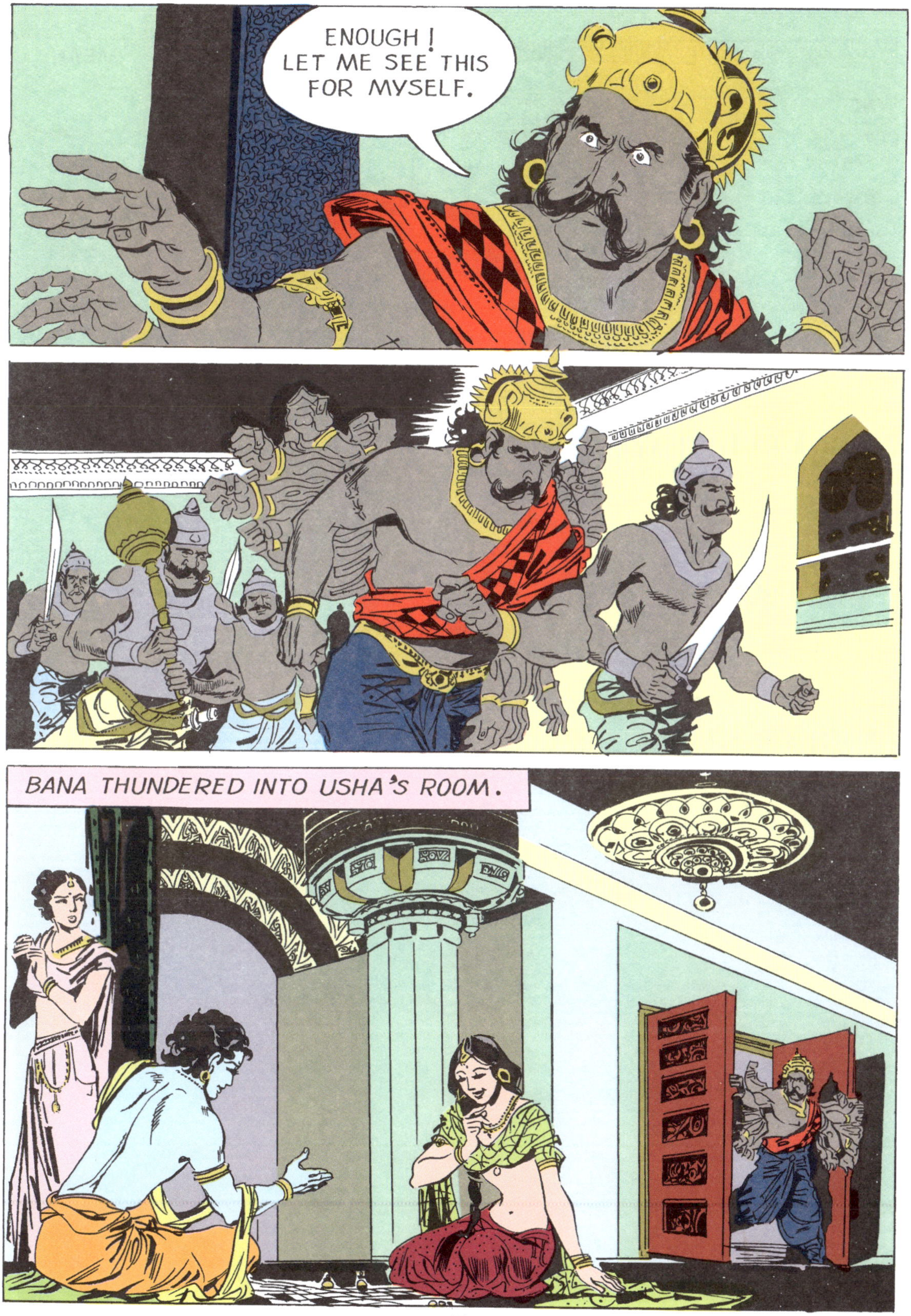
ENOUGH! LET ME SEE THIS FOR MYSELF.
BANA THUNDERED INTO USHA'S ROOM.

SEIZE HIM! KILL HIM!

BUT ANIRUDDHA WAS QUICK. HE GRABBED A MACE FROM ONE OF THE ATTENDANTS...

... AND SLEW ALL OF THEM BEFORE THEY COULD EVEN REALISE WHAT WAS HAPPENING.

BANA WAS LIVID WITH RAGE.

USHA, LEAVE THE CHAMBER, AND DON'T LET ME SEE YOUR FACE.
BANA HELD ANIRUDDHA WITH SOME OF HIS THOUSAND ARMS AND WITH OTHERS HE BOUND HIM FROM HEAD TO FOOT, USING SERPENTS FOR ROPES.
CHITRALEKHA, WHO SAW ALL THAT HAPPENED, RAN TO USHA.

HAS MY FATHER KILLED HIM ?
NO ! HE HAS...

...BOUND HIM FROM HEAD TO TOE WITH LIVE SERPENTS !
OH ! OH ! WHY DID I EVER ASK YOU TO BRING HIM HERE.

MEANWHILE ALL DWARAKA WAS UPSET ABOUT THE DISAPPEARANCE OF ANIRUDDHA.
FOUR MONTHS HAVE PASSED AND THERE IS NO TRACE OF HIM.
WHAT COULD HAVE HAPPENED TO HIM ?

KRISHNA HAS SENT FOR SAGE NARADA.
HAS HE ?
HE IS SURE TO KNOW WHERE ANIRUDDHA IS.
NARADA CAME TO SEE KRISHNA, AND CAME WITH NEWS.
ANIRUDDHA IS IN THE COURT OF BANA. BANA HAS BOUND HIM WITH LIVE SERPENTS AND IMPRISONED HIM.

KRISHNA CALLED A COUNCIL OF ALL HIS MEN.
GET YOUR HORSES, CHARIOTS AND ARMS READY FOR BATTLE. ANIRUDDHA IS ALIVE, BUT IN DANGER. I HAVE JUST HAD NEWS OF HIM.

KRISHNA, PRADYUMNA AND SATYAKI WITH HUNDREDS OF WARRIORS SET OUT FOR BANA'S KINGDOM TO RESCUE ANIRUDDHA.

WHEN THEY REACHED, KRISHNA GAVE THE COMMAND.
ATTACK!

BANA'S RAGE KNEW NO BOUNDS HE CAME OUT WITH AN EQUALLY LARGE ARMY AND A GREAT BATTLE ENSUED.

SHIVA WHO HAD PROMISED BANA HIS PROTECTION AT ALL TIMES, CAME TO HIS AID, WITH HIS SON, KARTIKEYA.

KRISHNA FOUGHT WITH SHIVA...

...PRADYUMNA WITH KARTIKEYA...

... AND SATYAKI WITH BANA.

ALL THE CELESTIALS, HEADED BY BRAHMA, THE SAGES, THE GANDHARVAS, THE APSARAS AND YAKSHAS CAME IN THEIR CHARIOTS TO WATCH THE MIGHTY BATTLE.
KRISHNA WAS EASILY THE BEST WARRIOR. IN NO TIME AT ALL HE DESTROYED SHIVA'S WEIRD HORDES WITH THE HELP OF JRIMBHANASTRA WHICH KEPT SHIVA STUPEFIED.

PRADYUMNA VANQUISHED KARTIKEYA WITH EASE.
BANA WAS BLIND WITH ANGER. HE LEFT SATYAKI...
...AND RUSHED AT KRISHNA.
SHIVA'S CURSE LIES HEAVY UPON ME NOW. BUT I WILL NOT GIVE UP HOPE.

WITH HIS THOUSAND ARMS, HE DREW FIVE HUNDRED BOWS AT THE SAME TIME AND SET TWO ARROWS IN EACH.

BUT KRISHNA WAS TOO QUICK FOR HIM. WITH HIS DISCUS HE CUT OFF NINE HUNDRED AND NINETY-SIX OF BANA'S ARMS, KILLED HIS CHARIOTEER AND HORSES, AND DESTROYED HIS CHARIOT.

AND THEN HE BLEW HIS CONCH IN TRIUMPH.

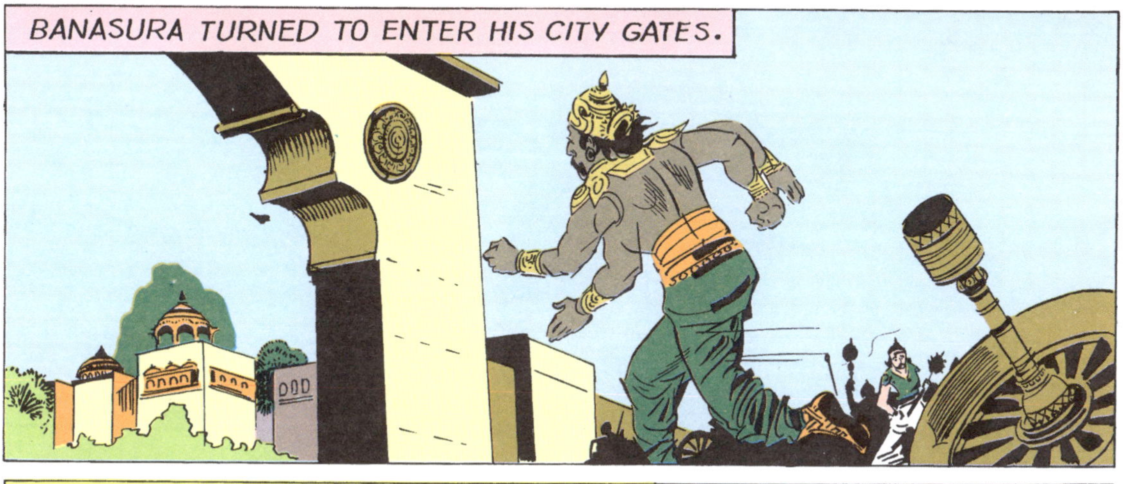
BANASURA TURNED TO ENTER HIS CITY GATES.

KRISHNA WAS ABOUT TO FOLLOW WHEN—
KRISHNA, BANA IS DEVOTED TO ME AND I HAVE PROMISED HIM MY PROTECTION.

I PLEAD WITH YOU TO SPARE HIM.

KRISHNA SMILED AT SHIVA.
IT IS ONLY TO HUMBLE HIM THAT I HAVE CUT OFF ALL EXCEPT FOUR OF HIS ARMS.

AND TO RELIEVE THE EARTH OF HER BURDEN, I HAVE DESTROYED HIS ARMY.
HE STILL HAS FOUR ARMS LEFT. BESIDES I GRANT HIM IMMORTALITY AND EVERLASTING-ING YOUTH.

HE NEED FEAR NO ONE.
SHIVA TURNED TO ONE OF HIS SURVIVING FOLLOWERS.
BRING BANA TO US.
KRISHNA HAS PARDONED AS WELL AS BLESSED YOU. BRING HIS GRANDSON AND YOUR DAUGHTER TO HIM.
BANA LEFT THEM AND RETURNED WITH USHA AND ANIRUDDHA.

ALL DWARAKA IS ANXIOUS FOR THE RETURN OF ANIRUDDHA. WE SHALL SET OFF IMMEDIATELY.

THEN, PLACING USHA AND ANIRUDDHA IN FRONT OF HIM, THE VICTORIOUS KRISHNA, ALONG WITH PRADYUMNA AND SATYAKI, RETURNED TO DWARAKA.